~ THIS ~

BOOK BELONGS

~ TO ~

....

....

....

~THE~
PUFFIN
BEDTIME
TREASURY

VIKING/PUFFIN

Published by the Penguin Group
Penguin Books Ltd, 27 Wrights Lane, London W8 5TZ, England
Penguin Putnam Inc., 375 Hudson Street, New York, New York 10014, USA
Penguin Books Australia Ltd, Ringwood, Victoria, Australia
Penguin Books Canada Ltd, 10 Alcorn Avenue, Toronto, Ontario, Canada M4V 3B2
Penguin Books (NZ) Ltd, Private Bag 102902, NSMC, Auckland, New Zealand

On the World Wide Web at: www.penguin.com

Penguin Books Ltd, Registered Offices: Harmondsworth, Middlesex, England

First published 2000
1 3 5 7 9 10 8 6 4 2

Made and printed in Italy by de Agostini

British Library Cataloguing in Publication Data
A CIP catalogue record for this book is available from the British Library

ISBN 0–670–89127–4

~THE~
PUFFIN
BEDTIME
TREASURY

PUFFIN BOOKS

ACKNOWLEDGEMENTS

The publishers gratefully acknowledge the following for permission to reproduce copyright material. Every effort has been made to trace copyright holders, but in some cases have proved impossible. The publishers would be happy to hear from any copyright holder that has not been acknowledged.

A Kiss Like This by Catherine and Laurence Anholt, first published by Hamish Hamilton 1997, revised edition published in Puffin Books 1999, copyright © Laurence and Catherine Anholt, reprinted by kind permission of the authors; 'The Song of the Daisy Fairy' and 'The Song of the Old-Man's-Beard Fairy' by Cicely Mary Barker, copyright © the Estate of Cicely Mary Barker, 1923, 1926, reproduced by permission of Frederick Warne & Co., illustrations by Cicely Mary Barker, copyright © Cicely Mary Barker, 1923, 1926, 1990, reproduced by permission of Frederick Warne & Co.; 'I Never See the Stars at Night' from *Aylsham Fair* by George Barker, published by Faber and Faber Limited, reproduced by permission of the publishers; 'Full Moon' from *The Complete Poems of Walter de la Mare* (1969), reprinted by permission of The Literary Trustees of Walter de la Mare, and the Society of Authors as their representative; 'Cats' from *The Children's Bells* by Eleanor Farjeon, published by Oxford University Press, reprinted by permission of David Higham Associates Limited; 'And That's All' from *Peculiar Rhymes and Lunatic Lines* by Max Fatchen, first published in the UK by Orchard Books in 1995, a division of The Watts Publishing Group Limited, 96 Leonard Street, London EC2A 4XD; *Sweet Dreams, Spot* by Eric Hill copyright © Eric Hill, 1998, this presentation 2000, reproduced by permission of Ventura Publishing; 'Vespers' from *When We Were Very Young* published by Methuen 1924, copyright © A. A. Milne, 1924, reprinted by permission of Egmont Children's Books Limited, London, illustrations by E. H. Shepard copyright under the Berne Conventions and in the USA copyright 1924 by E. P. Dutton, copyright renewal 1952 by A. A. Milne, colouring copyright © Dutton Children's Books USA, a member of Penguin Putnam, Inc. and used with permission; 'Sweet Dreams' from *Verses From 1929 On* by Ogden Nash, copyright © 1961, 1962 by Ogden Nash, reprinted by permission of Little, Brown and Company (Inc.).; *The Tale of the Flopsy Bunnies* by Beatrix Potter, copyright © Frederick Warne & Co., 1909, 1987, reproduced by permission of Frederick Warne & Co.; 'Summer Stars' from *Smoke and Steel* by Carl Sandburg, reprinted by permission of Harcourt, Inc.; 'Man in the Moon' from *Tickle My Nose* by Kaye Umansky, published in Puffin Books, 1999, copyright © Kaye Umansky 1999, reprinted by permission of Penguin Books Ltd.; *The Elephant and the Bad Baby* by Elfrida Vipont, first published by Hamish Hamilton 1969, revised edition published in Puffin 1971, copyright © Elfrida Vipont Foulds, 1969, reprinted by kind permission of Mrs C. Shaw on behalf of the Estate of Elfrida Vipont, illustrations copyright © Raymond Briggs, 1969, reprinted by kind permission of Raymond Briggs; *Goo-goo Gorilla* by Ian Whybrow, first published by Viking in 1998, revised edition published in Puffin 1999, copyright © Ian Whybrow, reprinted by permission of the author, illustrations copyright © Tony Blundell, reprinted by kind permission of the Caroline Sheldon Literary Agency on behalf of the illustrator; 'Mermaid's Lullaby', first published in *Dragon Night and Other Lullabies* by Methuen, copyright © 1980 by Jane Yolen, reprinted by permission of Curtis Brown, Ltd.

Contents

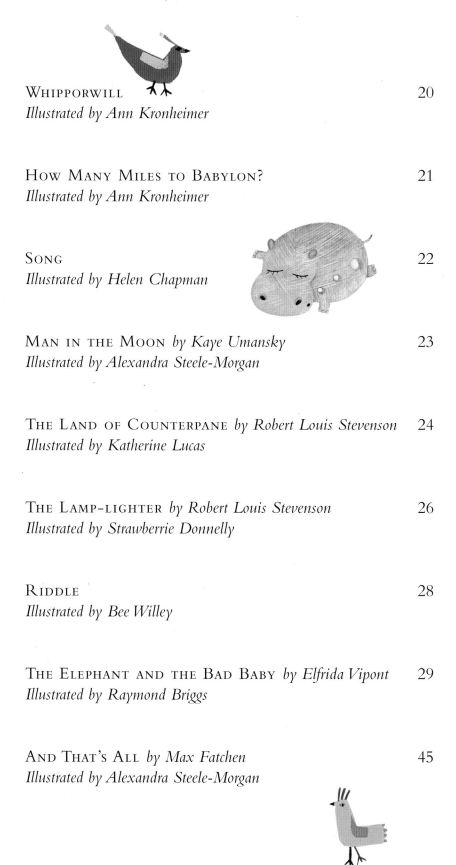

Lullaby

Bed is too small for my tired head,
Give me a hill soft with leaves.
Tuck a cloud up under my chin,
Lord, blow the moon out – please!

Rock me to sleep in a cradle of leaves,
Sing me a lullaby of dreams.
Tuck a cloud up under my chin,
Lord, blow the moon out – please!

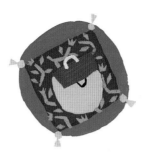

ℬED

Go to bed first,
A golden purse;
Go to bed second,
A golden pheasant;
Go to bed third,
A golden bird.

BEDTIME

Down with the lambs
Up with the lark,
Run to bed, children,
Before it gets dark.

Wynken, Blynken and Nod

Wynken, Blynken and Nod one night
Sailed off in a wooden shoe –
Sailed on a river of crystal light,
Into a sea of dew.
"Where are you going, and what do you wish?"
The old moon asked the three.
"We have come to fish the herring fish
That live in this beautiful sea;
Nets of silver and gold have we!"
Said Wynken,
Blynken
And Nod.

The old moon laughed and sang a song,
As they rocked in the wooden shoe,
And the wind that sped them all night long
Ruffled with waves of dew.
The little stars were the herring fish
That lived in that beautiful sea –
"Now cast your nets wherever you wish –
Never afeared are we,"
So cried the stars to the fishermen three:
Wynken,
Blyknen
And Nod.

All night long their nets they threw
To the stars in the twinkling foam –
Then down from the skies came the wooden shoe,
Bringing the fishermen home;
'Twas all so pretty a sail it seemed
As if it could not be,
And some folks thought 'twas a dream they'd dreamed
Of sailing that beautiful sea –
But I shall name you the fishermen three:
Wynken,
Blynken
And Nod.

Wynken and Blynken are two little eyes,
And Nod is a little head,
And the wooden shoe that sailed to the skies
Is a wee one's trundle bed.
So shut your eyes while your mother sings
Of wonderful sights that be,
And you shall see the beautiful things
As you rock in the misty sea,
Where the old shoe rocked and the fishermen three,
Wynken,
Blynken
And Nod.

Eugene Field

THE SONG OF THE OLD MAN'S-BEARD FAIRY

This is where the little elves
Cuddle down to hide themselves;
Into fluffy beds they creep,
Say good-night, and go to sleep.

Cicely Mary Barker

Lullaby
and Goodnight

Lullaby and goodnight,
With roses delight,
With lilies bespread
Is baby's wee bed.
Lay thee down now and rest,
May thy slumber be blest.
Lay thee down now and rest,
May thy slumber be blest.

Lullaby and goodnight,
Thy mother's delight,
Bright angels around
My darling shall stand;
They will guard thee from harms,
Thou shalt wake in my arms,
They will guard thee from harms,
Thou shalt wake in my arms.

Fritz Simrock

My Candle

My candle burns at both ends;
It will not last the night.
But ah, my foes and oh, my friends –
It gives a lovely light!

Edna St Vincent Millay

Sweet Dreams, Spot

Eric Hill

It was the start of a busy day.
After breakfast, Spot went with his mum
to do the shopping. There was a long list
of things to get.

"Thank you, Spot,"
said Sally.
"I couldn't have
done all this
without your help."

After lunch, he went to the park with his dad. "Come on, Spot," said Sam. "I'll race you to the playground."

At the playground, Spot went on the swings. "Push me higher, Dad!" said Spot.

When Spot and his dad got home from the park, Helen, Tom and Steve came over to play hide-and-seek.

Finally, as it was getting dark, Spot's friends went home to bed.
Spot was ready for bed too.

After Spot had had his supper, he went for a last walk in the garden.

A small voice said, "Hello, Spot, have you come out to play?"
"No, I'm going to bed," said Spot.
"Oh well," said the mole, "sleep tight."

As Spot walked by the pond, he heard a frog croak.
"Hello, Spot. It's a lovely evening for a swim."
"Not for me, thanks. I'm off to bed,"
said Spot.

"Tu-whit, tu-whoo!" hooted
the owl.
"Good-night, Owl," said Spot.
"What do you mean *good-night?*"
the owl asked. "I've just woken
up. I've got lots to do."
"Rather you than me," Spot yawned.
"I've had a busy day."

Spot went back indoors.
"Good-night, everyone," he said.
"Have fun!"

Spot kissed his dad. "I've had
a lovely day, Dad. Thanks for
taking me to the park."
"Good-night, Spot," said Sam.

Sally came in to kiss Spot good-night.
"Read me a story, Mum," said Spot.
Sally opened the book and started to read.

Spot snuggled down, cosy
and warm. He got sleepier
and sleepier. By the time
the story was over, Spot
was fast asleep.

18

"What a tired little puppy you were," Sally whispered.
"I didn't realize that you were already asleep. I've been
reading this story and there was no one listening."
"Oh yes there was," said a voice.
Sally looked round and there sitting on the window-sill
were the owl, the frog and the mole.

"Thanks for the story, Sally,"
they said. "And sweet
dreams, Spot."
Spot opened one eye.
"Yes, thanks, Mum," he said.
"Good-night, everyone."
And he fell fast asleep again.

WHIPPORWILL

Gone to bed is the setting sun,
Night is coming and day is done.
Whipporwill, whipporwill,
Has just begun.

HOW MANY MILES TO BABYLON?

How many miles to Babylon?
Three score miles and ten.
Will we get there by candlelight?
Yes, if your feet are nimble and bright,
You will get there by candlelight.
There and back again.

21

SONG

Hush-a-bye, baby,
Daddy's away,
Brothers and sisters have gone out to play,
But here by your cradle,
Dear baby, I'll keep,
To guard you from danger
And sing you to sleep.

MAN IN THE MOON

Man in the moon,
See you soon,
Stars in the sky,
Goodbye, goodbye,
Off with the light,
Night, night,
See you in the morning.

Kaye Umanksy

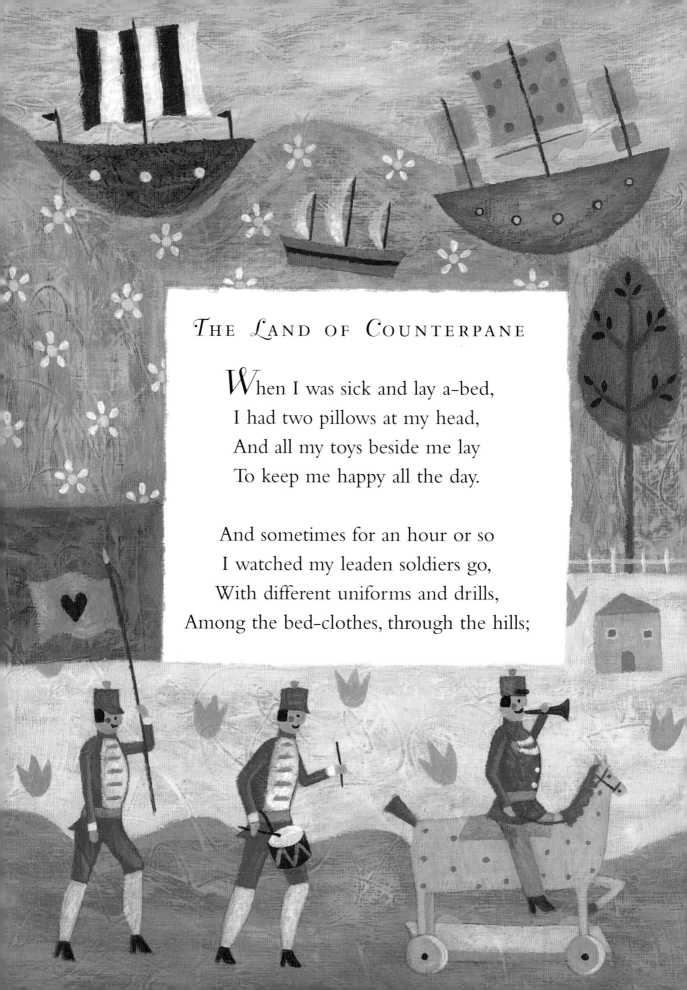

The Land of Counterpane

When I was sick and lay a-bed,
I had two pillows at my head,
And all my toys beside me lay
To keep me happy all the day.

And sometimes for an hour or so
I watched my leaden soldiers go,
With different uniforms and drills,
Among the bed-clothes, through the hills;

And sometimes sent my ships in fleets
All up and down among the sheets;
Or brought my trees and houses out,
And planted cities all about.

I was the giant great and still
That sits upon the pillow-hill,
And sees before him, dale and plain,
The pleasant land of counterpane.

Robert Louis Stevenson

THE LAMP-LIGHTER

My tea is nearly ready and the sun has left the sky;
It's time to take the window to see Leerie going by;
For every night at tea-time and before you take your seat,
With lantern and with ladder he comes posting up the street.

Now Tom would be a driver and Maria go to sea,
And my papa's a banker and as rich as he can be;
But I, when I am stronger and can choose what I'm to do,
O Leerie, I'll go round at night and light the lamps with you!

For we are very lucky, with a lamp before the door,
And Leerie stops to light it as he lights so many more;
And O! before you hurry by with ladder and with light,
O Leerie, see a little child and nod to him tonight!

Robert Louis Stevenson

RIDDLE

Little Nancy Etticoat,
With a white petticoat,
And a red nose;
She has no feet or hands,
The longer she stands
The shorter she grows.

(answer – a candle)

The Elephant
and the
Bad Baby

by Elfrida Vipont

Illustrated by Raymond Briggs

Once upon a time there was an Elephant.
And one day the Elephant went for a walk and
he met a Bad Baby. And the Elephant said
to the Bad Baby,

"Would you like a ride?" And the Bad Baby said,
"Yes." So the Elephant stretched out his trunk, and picked
up the Bad Baby and put him on his back, and they went
rumpeta, rumpeta, rumpeta, all down the road.

Very soon they met an ice-cream man.
And the Elephant said to the Bad Baby,
"Would you like an ice-cream?" And the Bad Baby
said, "Yes." So the Elephant stretched out his trunk and
took an ice-cream for himself and an ice-cream for the
Bad Baby, and they went rumpeta, rumpeta, rumpeta,
all down the road, with the ice-cream
man running after.

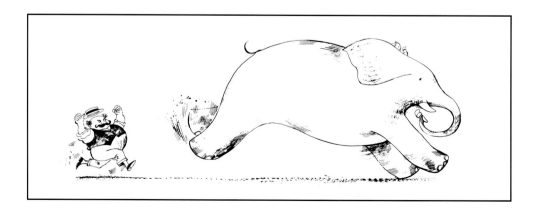

Next they came to a pork butcher's shop.
And the Elephant said to the Bad Baby,
"Would you like a pie?" And the Bad Baby said, "Yes." So
the Elephant stretched out his trunk and took a pie for
himself and a pie for the Bad Baby, and they went
rumpeta, rumpeta, rumpeta, all down the road, with
the ice-cream man and the pork butcher
both running after.

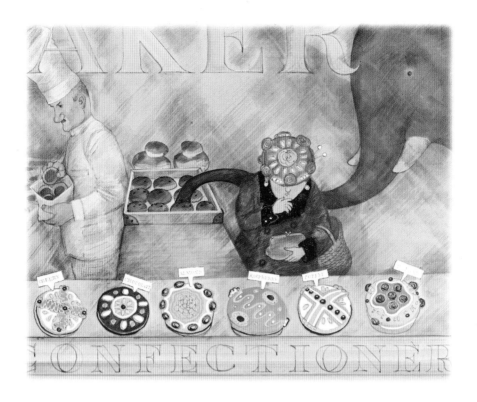

Next they came to a baker's shop. And the Elephant
said to the Bad Baby, "Would you like a bun?"
And the Bad Baby said, "Yes." So the Elephant stretched
out his trunk and took a bun for himself and a bun
for the Bad Baby, and they went rumpeta, rumpeta,
rumpeta, all down the road, with the ice-cream man,
and the pork butcher, and the baker
all running after.

Next they came to a snack bar. And the Elephant said to the Bad Baby, "Would you like some crisps?" And the Bad Baby said, "Yes." So the Elephant stretched out his trunk and took some crisps for himself and some crisps for the Bad Baby, and they went rumpeta, rumpeta, rumpeta, all down the road, with the ice-cream man and the pork butcher, and the baker, and the snack-bar man all running after.

Next they came to a grocer's shop. And the Elephant said
to the Bad Baby, "Would you like a chocolate biscuit?"
And the Bad Baby said, "Yes." So the Elephant stretched
out his trunk and took a chocolate biscuit for himself and
a chocolate biscuit for the Bad Baby, and they went
rumpeta, rumpeta, rumpeta, all down the road, with the
ice-cream man and the pork butcher, and the baker, and
the snack-bar man and the grocer all running after.

Next they came to a sweet shop. And the Elephant said
to the Bad Baby, "Would you like a lollipop?" And the
Bad Baby said, "Yes." So the Elephant stretched out his
trunk and took a lollipop for himself and a lollipop for the
Bad Baby, and they went rumpeta, rumpeta, rumpeta, all
down the road, with the ice-cream man and the pork
butcher, and the baker, and the snack-bar man and the
grocer, and the lady from the sweet shop all running after.

Next they came to a fruit barrow.

And the Elephant said to the Bad Baby, "Would you like
an apple?" And the Bad Baby said, "Yes." So the Elephant
stretched out his trunk and took an apple for himself and
an apple for the Bad Baby, and they went rumpeta,
rumpeta, rumpeta, all down the road, with the ice-cream
man and the pork butcher, and the baker, and the
snack-bar man, and the grocer, and the lady from the
sweet shop, and the barrow boy all running after.

Then the Elephant said to the Bad Baby, "But you haven't once said please!" And then he said, "You haven't ONCE said please!" Then the Elephant sat down suddenly in the middle of the road and the Bad Baby fell off.

And the ice-cream man, and the pork butcher, and the baker, and the snack-bar man, and the grocer, and the lady from the sweet shop, and the barrow boy all went BUMP into a heap.

And the Elephant said, "But he never once said please!"
And the ice-cream man, and the pork butcher, and the
baker, and the snack-bar man, and the grocer, and the lady
from the sweet shop, and the barrow boy all picked
themselves up and said, "Just fancy that! He never once
said please!" And the Bad Baby said: "PLEASE! I want to
go home to my Mummy!"

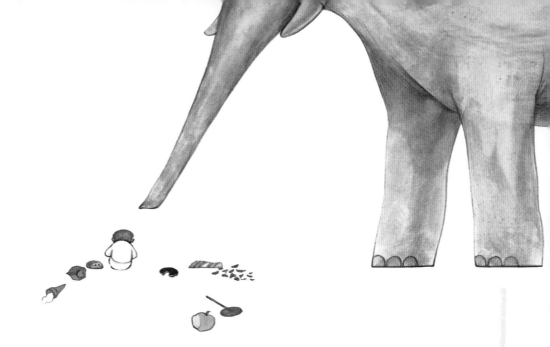

So the Elephant stretched out his trunk, and picked up the
Bad Baby and put him on his back, and they went
rumpeta, rumpeta, rumpeta, all down the road, with the
ice-cream man and the pork butcher, and the baker, and
the snack-bar man, and the grocer, and the lady from the
sweet shop, and the barrow boy all running after.

When the Bad Baby's Mummy saw them, she said, "Have you come for tea?" And they all said, "Yes, *please!*"

So they all went in and had tea, and the Bad Baby's
Mummy made pancakes for everybody.

Then the Elephant went rumpeta, rumpeta, rumpeta, all down the road, with the ice-cream man, and the pork butcher, and the baker, and the snack-bar man, and the grocer, and the lady from the sweet shop, and the barrow boy all running after.

And the Bad Baby went to bed.

AND THAT'S ALL

A happy day
Is precious to keep,
So take it to bed
And wrap it in sleep.

Max Fatchen

TWINKLE, TWINKLE, LITTLE STAR

Twinkle, twinkle, little star,
How I wonder what you are.
Up above the world so high,
Like a diamond in the sky.
Twinkle, twinkle, little star,
How I wonder what you are.

When the blazing sun is set,
When the grass with dew is wet,
Then you show your little light,
Twinkle, twinkle, all the night.
Twinkle, twinkle, little star,
How I wonder what you are.

Then the traveller in the dark,
Thanks you for the tiny spark
He could not see which way to go,
If you did not twinkle so.
Though I know not what you are,
Twinkle, twinkle, little star.

WEE WILLIE WINKIE

Wee Willie Winkie
Runs through the town,
Upstairs and downstairs
In his night-gown.
Rapping at the window,
Crying through the lock,
"Are all the children in their beds,
It's now eight o'clock?"

HUSH-A-BYE

Hush-a-bye, baby,
Pussy's a lady,
Mousie has gone to the mill;
And if you don't cry
She'll come back by and by,
So hush-a-bye, baby, lie still.

CATS

Cats sleep
Anywhere,
Any table,
Any chair,
Top of piano,
Window-ledge,
In the middle,
On the edge,
Open drawer,
Empty shoe,

Anybody's
Lap will do,
Fitted in a
Cardboard box,
In a cupboard
With your frocks –
They don't care!
Cats sleep
Anywhere.

Eleanor Farjeon

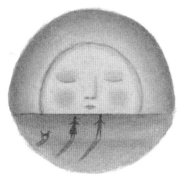

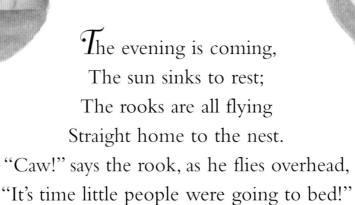

BEDTIME

The evening is coming,
The sun sinks to rest;
The rooks are all flying
Straight home to the nest.
"Caw!" says the rook, as he flies overhead,
"It's time little people were going to bed!"

The flowers are closing;
The daisy's asleep
The primrose is buried
In slumber so deep.
Shut up for the night is the pimpernel red;
It's time little people were going to bed!

The butterfly, drowsy,
Has folded its wing;
The bees are returning,
No more the birds sing.
Their labour is over, their nestlings are fed;
It's time little people were going to bed!

Here comes the pony,
His work is all done;
Down through the meadow
He takes a good run;
Up go his heels and down goes his head;
It's time little people were going to bed!

Good night, little people,
Good night and good night;
Sweet dreams to your eyelids
Till dawning of light;
The evening has come, there's no more to be said,
It's time little people were going to bed!

Thomas Hood

GOOD NIGHT

*H*ere's a body – there's a bed!
There's a pillow – here's a head!
There's a curtain – here's a light!
There's a puff – and so good night!

Thomas Hood

Banyan Tree

Moonshine tonight, come mek we dance and sing,
Moonshine tonight, come mek we dance and sing,
Me deh rock so, yu deh rock so, under banyan tree,
Me deh rock so, yu deh rock so, under banyan tree.

SWEET AND LOW

Sweet and low, sweet and low,
Wind of the western sea,
Low, low, breathe and blow,
Wind of the western sea!
Over the rolling waters go,
Come from the dying moon, and blow,
Blow him again to me;
While my little one, while my pretty one, sleeps.

Sleep and rest, sleep and rest,
Father will come to thee soon;
Rest, rest, on mother's breast,
Father will come to thee soon;
Father will come to his babe in the nest,
Silver sails all out of the west
Under the silver moon;
Sleep, my little one, sleep, my pretty one, sleep.

Alfred, Lord Tennyson

HUSH-YOU-BYE

Hush-you-bye,
Don't you cry,
Go to sleep, my little baby.
When you wake,
You shall have cake,
An' drive those pretty little horses.

Rock-a-bye,
Don't you cry,
Go to sleep, my little baby.
Send you to school
Ridin' on a mule
An' driving those pretty little horses,
Blacks an' bays,
Dapples an' greys,
Coach an' six-a little horses.

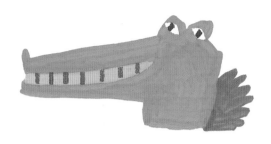

Ten in the Bed

There were ten in the bed
And the little one said,
"Roll over, roll over."
So they all rolled over
And one fell out …

There were nine in the bed
And the little one said,
"Roll over, roll over."
So they all rolled over
And one fell out …

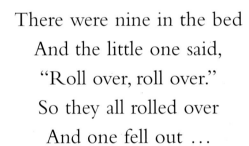

There were eight in the bed
And the little one said,
"Roll over, roll over."
So they all rolled over
And one fell out …

There were seven in the bed
And the little one said,
"Roll over, roll over."
So they all rolled over
And one fell out …

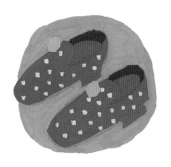

There were six in the bed
And the little one said,
"Roll over, roll over."
So they all rolled over
And one fell out …

There were five in the bed
And the little one said,
"Roll over, roll over."
So they all rolled over
And one fell out …

There were four in the bed
And the little one said,
"Roll over, roll over."
So they all rolled over
And one fell out …

There were three in the bed
And the little one said,
"Roll over, roll over."
So they all rolled over
And one fell out …

There were two in the bed
And the little one said,
"Roll over, roll over."
So they all rolled over
And one fell out …

There was one in the bed
And the little one said,
"Good morning!"

SLEEPING OUTDOORS

Under the dark
Is a star,
Under the star
Is a tree,
Under the tree
Is a blanket,
And under the
Blanket is me.

Marchette Chute

A Prayer

Matthew, Mark, Luke and John,
Bless the bed that I lie on.
Four corners to my bed,
Four angels round my head,
One to watch, one to pray,
Two to bear my soul away.

A Kiss Like This

Catherine & Laurence Anholt

When Little Cub was born,
Big Golden Lion just
couldn't stop kissing him.

"GRRRR!" he growled. "You're the most kissable cub in the world."

Big Golden Lion kissed Little Cub behind
his prickly ears . . . *just like this.*

And Little Cub giggled.

He kissed Little Cub on the end of his
small pink nose . . . *just like this.*

And Little Cub wriggled.

He kissed Little Cub right on his warm fat
tummy and blew a raspberry on his
belly button …

just like this.

And Little Cub giggled and wriggled and
jiggled.

In the golden evening
sunshine, Little Cub played outside.

Everyone who passed by and saw Little Cub
wanted to kiss him too.

They just couldn't help it.

Along came Jumpy Monkey

and gave Little Cub a tickly
monkey kiss behind his
prickly ears,

on the end of his small pink nose

and right in the middle of his warm fat
tummy …

just like this.

And Little Cub giggled and wriggled and
jiggled.

Along came Squawky Parrot

and gave Little Cub a pecky
parrot kiss behind his
prickly ears,

on the end of his
small pink nose

and right in the middle of his warm fat
tummy …

just like this.

And Little Cub giggled and wriggled and
jiggled even more.

Along came
Big Fat Rhino

and gave Little Cub a
nuzzling nosy rhino
kiss behind his
prickly ears,

on the end of his
small pink nose

and right in the middle of his warm fat
tummy ...

just like this.

And Little Cub giggled and wriggled and
jiggled all over again.

Along came Slippery Snake

and gave Little Cub a
s-s-slow hiss-s-sing
s-s-snake kiss-s-s
behind his prickly
ears-s-s,

on the end of his
small pink nos-s-se

and right in the middle of his warm fat tummy …

just like this-s-s.

And Little Cub giggled and wriggled and jiggled even more still.

Along came
Old Grey Elephant

and gave Little Cub a
slurpy sloppy elephant
kiss behind his
prickly ears,

on the end of his
small pink nose

and right in the middle of his warm fat
tummy …

just like this.

And Little Cub giggled and wriggled and
jiggled more than ever.

Then, last of all, along came Mean Green Hungry Crocodile snapping his wicked white teeth.

He saw Little Cub playing in the golden evening sunshine.

"Little Cub, you certainly are the most kissable cub in the world.

"Come over here and I will give you a snippy snappy crocodile kiss."

But Little Cub didn't want a snippy snappy
crocodile kiss at all. And he began to cry.

Mean Green Hungry Crocodile opened
his mean green hungry mouth and showed
all his wicked white crocodile teeth …

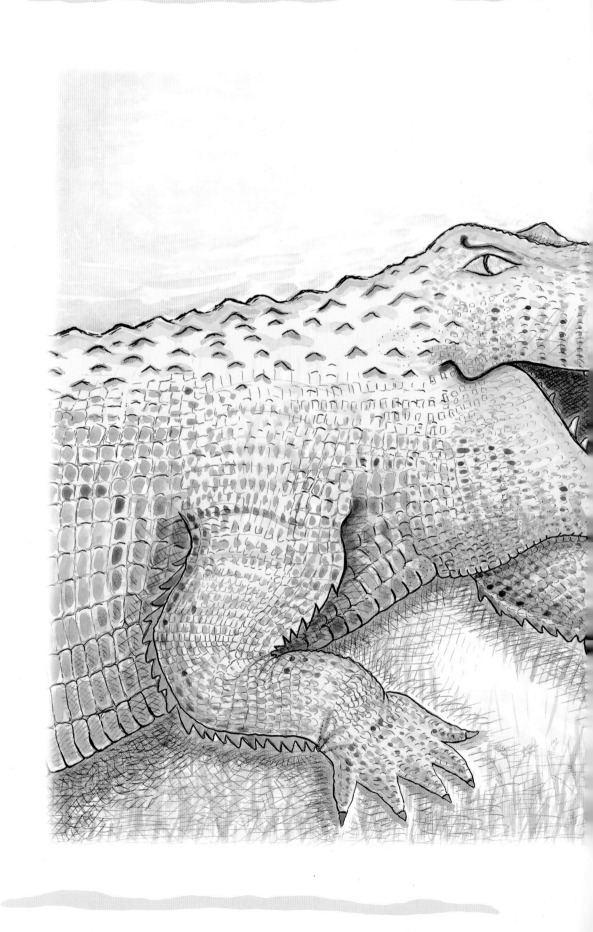

JUST
LIKE
THIS!

Quick as a flash, along came Big Golden

Lion and **ROARED** a Big

Golden Lion **ROAR** until Mean Green

Hungry Crocodile turned and ran away.

Big Golden Lion carried Little Cub back to
their safe warm home and tucked him into
his safe warm bed.

Then Big Golden Lion
stretched himself. "Listen,
Little Cub," he said.

"There's nothing better
than a tickly monkey kiss –
when you're a tiny monkey.

"And a parrot peck is
perfect – when you're
a baby parrot.

"No one loves a rhino
nuzzle quite like a
newborn rhino.

"A s-s-snake kiss-s-s is especially nic-c-ce – when you're a baby snake.

"And you can't have too many elephant kisses – when you're a little elephant.

"And *even* snippy snappy baby crocodiles love snippy snappy kisses."

"But", said Big Golden Lion, yawning, "when you're a sleepy Little Lion Cub, there's only one thing in the whole wide world that's completely, exactly right …"

And that's …

A HUGE GREAT
Big Golden Lion kiss ...

just like this!

SCARECROW

When all the cows were sleeping,
And the sun had gone to bed,
Up jumped the scarecrow,
And this is what he said:

"I'm a dingle dangle scarecrow,
With a flippy floppy hat,
I can shake my arms like this,
I can shake my legs like that."

GRANDMOTHER'S GLASSES

Here are Grandmother's glasses,
And here is Grandmother's hat,
And here's the way she folds her hands,
And puts them in her lap.

Here are Grandfather's glasses,
And here is Grandfather's hat,
And here's the way he folds his hands,
And has a little nap.

GRANNY'S GONE TO SLEEP

Granny's gone to sleep:
Softly, little boys;
Read your pretty books,
Don't make a noise.
Pussy's on the stool,
Quiet as a mouse;
Not a whisper runs
Through the whole house.
Hush! Silence keep;
Granny's gone to sleep.

Matthias Barr

Full Moon

One night as Dick lay half asleep,
Into his drowsy eyes
A great still light began to creep
From out the silent skies.
It was the lovely moon's, for when
He raised his dreamy head,
Her surge of silver filled the pane
And streamed across his bed.
So, for a while, each gazed at each –
Dick and the solemn moon –
Till, climbing slowly on her way,
She vanished and was gone.

Walter de la Mare

One o'Clock

One of the clock, and silence deep
Then up the stairway black and steep
The old house-cat comes creepy-creep
With soft feet goes from room to room
Her green eyes shining through the gloom
And finds all fast asleep.

Katharine Pyle

To Bed, to Bed

"To bed, to bed," cried Sleepy-head.
"Tarry awhile," said Slow.
Said Greedy Nan, "Put on the pan,
Let's dine before we go."

"To bed, to bed," cried Sleepy-head.
But all the rest said, "No!
It is morning now; you must milk the cow,
And tomorrow to bed we go."

THE PRINCESS AND THE PEA

Adapted from Hans Christian Andersen by Mary Finch

 Once upon a time there was a prince. He was a very handsome prince and his father and mother were a king and queen, so one day he would be a king. He wanted to get married but he also wanted to be quite sure that the lady he married was a princess. A real princess. So he set off to find one. He travelled far and wide looking for princesses. He found plenty, but somehow he didn't think that any of them were real princesses. He couldn't explain why but he just knew that none of them was right.

Sadly, he rode off home to his own kingdom.

"Did you find her?" his parents asked him eagerly.

"No," he said, and went off to his bedroom in a sulk.

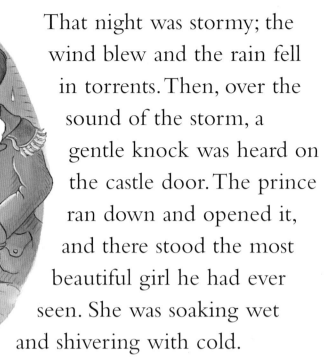

That night was stormy; the wind blew and the rain fell in torrents. Then, over the sound of the storm, a gentle knock was heard on the castle door. The prince ran down and opened it, and there stood the most beautiful girl he had ever seen. She was soaking wet and shivering with cold.

"Can I come in?" she asked through the chattering of her teeth. "I'm a princess and I've lost my way."

"Of course," said the prince. "Come in and get warm by the fire. Are you really a princess?" He hoped very much that she was, as he had fallen in love with her on the spot.

"Yes, I am," the princess answered, but the prince still had his doubts.

"You must stay the night," said the queen, coming down the stairs. She thought of a way of finding out whether the girl was a real princess. "Just sit here and have something to eat while I make up the spare bed."

The queen bustled off to the spare room, taking several servants with her. Together they made up the bed, not with just one mattress, but with ten mattresses, one on top of the other. Then the queen piled on not one quilt but ten quilts, and she added three fleecy blankets just in case. And underneath the very bottom mattress the queen had placed one small fresh pea.

"Would you like to go to bed now?" she asked the princess. And the princess, who was very tired, nodded her head and followed her. She was a little surprised when she saw how high the bed was, but the queen had leant a ladder against it so she could climb up easily.

The princess said goodnight to the queen and climbed into bed. She settled down but somehow she couldn't get comfortable. There seemed to be something lumpy under the mattresses. All night she tossed and turned, dozing a little, and she was very pleased when it was morning.

"How did you sleep?" asked the queen when the princess appeared at breakfast.

The princess was very polite and had been well brought up, but she had also been taught never to

tell a lie. "Terribly," she said. "I am covered in bruises. There was something hard and lumpy under the mattress, and I hardly slept a wink."

"Aha!" said the prince. "Now I know that you are a real princess. Only a real princess could have felt a pea through ten mattresses and ten quilts and three fleecy blankets! Will you marry me?"

The princess was again a little surprised, but she too had fallen in love with the prince the moment she had seen him, so she said yes. The prince and his real princess were married that day and lived happily ever after.

A CRADLE SONG

Sweet dreams form a shade,
O'er my lovely infant's head.
Sweet dreams of pleasant streams,
By happy silent moony beams.

William Blake

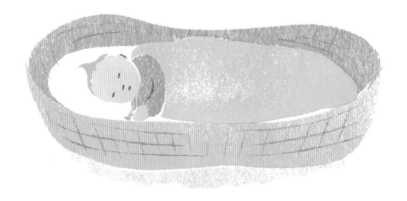

SWEET DREAMS

I wonder as into bed I creep
What it feels like to fall asleep.
I've told myself stories,
I've counted sheep,
But I'm always asleep when I fall asleep.
Tonight my eyes I will open keep,
And I'll stay awake till I fall asleep,
Then I'll know what it feels like to fall asleep,
Asleep,
Asleeep,
Asleeeep…

Ogden Nash

Mermaid's Lullaby

Hush, foam mocker,
Sleep, wave maker,
Close your eyes and dream,
Tide breaker.

Waves will rock you,
Whales will sing you,
Starfish a night-light
Will bring you.

Hush, deep diver,
Shush, shell keeper,
Be your finny mother's
Sleeper.

Jane Yolen

Prayer

Father–Mother God,
Loving me,
Guard me while I sleep,
Guide my little feet,
Up to thee.

Sleep, Sleep, Little One, Sleep

Sleep, sleep, little one, sleep.
There outside are all the sheep;
Lambs are penned up, safe from harm.
Sleep, my darling, cosy warm.
Sleep, sleep, little one, sleep.

Sleep, sleep, little one, sleep.
Guardian angels watch will keep;
There beneath the apple tree
Gather they sweet dreams for thee.
Sleep, sleep, little one, sleep.

Sleep, sleep, little one, sleep.
See the sky is filled with sheep;
Like a flock the clouds drift by,
Led by moonlit lullaby.
Sleep, sleep, little one, sleep.

113

JACK

Jack be nimble,
Jack be quick.
Jack jump over
The candlestick.

GOO-GOO GORILLA

Ian Whybrow

Illustrated by Tony Blundell

Once upon a treetop, there were three gorillas. They were Great Big Poppa Gorilla, Middle-size Momma Gorilla and Goo-goo the baby gorilla.

Every day, Great Big Poppa Gorilla, Middle-size Momma Gorilla and Goo-goo the baby gorilla went for a walk.

And when they reached the river bank, everyone stopped to admire the baby. All the warthogs stopped wallowing and they said,

WOW!

All the
hippopotamuses
stopped yawning
and they said,

All the crocodiles stopped crunching and they said,

And then all
the animals
said together:

And when they got to the park, Goo-goo went
on the swing.

All the rhinos stopped roundabouting and they said,

RING-A-DING! LOOK AT HIM SWING!

And all the snakes stopped sliding and they said,

And the tigers stopped see-sawing and they said,

And then all the animals said together:

Great Big Poppa Gorilla and Middle-size Momma Gorilla were so proud of Baby Goo-goo!

He smiled at all the mummy and daddy animals. He waved at all the granny and grandad animals.

He played peep-bo with all the little animals. All day long, he was a GOOD little Goo-goo Goriila.

124

But when it was time
to say night-night, he
was always overtired.
So at bedtime, Goo-goo
was a BAD baby gorilla.

He banged his plate
on the table.
He threw things about
in the bathroom.

"WAA-WAA-WAA!"

And when he
went to bed,
he went,

125

All through the forest, the animals tried to cover their ears.

But it was no good.
Nobody could get to sleep.

So one sleepless night, all the animals went to see the lion. "You're the king of the jungle," they said. "Can't you do something to stop that noise?"

So the lion went to see Momma Gorilla, and he growled and said, "GRRRahhh! This must stop. Sing Baby Goo-goo a lullaby!"

So very, very gently
Momma Gorilla took
Goo-goo in her arms,
and very, very gently
she rocked him, and
very, very quietly
she sang this lullaby:

High in the treetops, tucked up tight,
Baby gorilla is ready for the night.
Tiptoe through the jungle — gently, gently creep,
Momma sing a lullaby to rock him off to sleep.

WAA-WAA-WAA!

But Goo-goo went,
"WAA-WAA WAA!"
even louder and kept
all the animals awake.

129

"I know what to do," said the lioness. So she went to see Poppa Gorilla, and she growled and said, "GRRRahhh! This must stop. You sing Goo-goo a lullaby – and this time, even quieter."

So very, very, very gently Great Big Poppa Gorilla took Goo-goo in his arms, and very, very, very gently he rocked him, and very, very, very quietly he sang this lullaby:

High in the treetops, tucked up tight,
Baby gorilla is ready for the night.
Slowly, slowly close your eyes and do not peep –
Baby gorilla is falling asleep.

But Goo-goo went,
"waa-waa-waa!"
even louder and
kept all the
animals awake.

And they
groaned and they
gruffed and they
yawned and they
yuffed and they
thought they
would never get
to sleep.

"I know what to do," said the little lion cub. And all the animals stopped groaning and gruffing and yawning and yuffing and they said,

I BEG YOUR PARDON?

"That's not the way baby gorillas like lullabies," said the lion cub. "Well, how DO baby gorillas like lullabies?" said Momma Gorilla and Poppa Gorilla. "I'll whisper," said the shy little lion cub.

And he whispered.
And right away Middle-size Momma Gorilla grabbed Goo-goo in her great big hands and gave him a great big squeeze and rocked him in her great big arms and sang in her great big, rough, voice:

OO–OO, BABY BOO!
SQUEEZE, SQUEEZE, LOOK FOR FLEAS!
ROUGH, ROUGH, THAT'S ENOUGH!
GOO–GOO, OFF YOU GO —
GO TO SLEEP, GORILLA!

And Goo-goo stopped crying. And he laughed. And he said "AGAIN!" So Great Big Poppa Gorilla grabbed Goo-goo in his huge, great big hands and gave him a huge, great big squeeze and rocked him in his huge, great big arms and sang in his huge, great big, ROUGH voice:

OO-OO, BABY BOO!
SQUEEZE, SQUEEZE, LOOK FOR FLEAS!
ROUGH, ROUGH, THAT'S ENOUGH!
GOO-GOO, OFF YOU GO —
GO TO SLEEP, GORILLA!

And Goo-goo didn't say anything, because the lion cub was right. That is the way baby gorillas like lullabies.

And all the animals smiled and sighed with relief, because Goo-goo the baby gorilla was …

... fast asleep.

Sssssshhhh!!

Now the Day is Over

Now the day is over,
Night is drawing nigh;
Shadows of the evening
Steal across the sky.

Now the darkness gathers,
Stars begin to peep;
Birds and beasts and flowers
Soon will be asleep.

Father, give the weary
Calm and sweet repose;
With thy tender blessing,
May our eyelids close.

Through the long night-watches
May thine angels spread
Their white wings above me,
Watching around my bed.

Sabine Baring-Gould

Suliram – Go to Sleep

Go to sleep, go to sleep, sleep, sleep.
Go to sleep, little one.
Close your eyes and dream tender dreams,
For you are guarded, protected by my love.

Now go to sleep, go to sleep, sleep, sleep.
Go to sleep, little one.
Close your eyes and dream tender dreams,
For you are guarded, protected by my love.

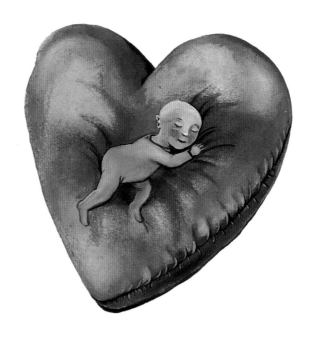

Long have I waited, I've waited for you.
(Go to sleep.)
Years I spent hoping and praying for you.
(Go to sleep.)
Now that I have you right here by my side,
I will not ever, no, never let you go.

Now go to sleep, go to sleep, sleep, sleep…

Time for Bed

Baby mine, O baby mine,
Now go to sleep;
Close your little sleepy eyes
And dream sweet dreams.

Dodo, petit po-po,
Mamma coming just now;
Dodo, petit po-po,
Mamma coming just now.

Afro-Caribbean, collected by Grace Hallworth

Girls and Boys Come Out to Play

Girls and boys, come out to play,
The moon doth shine bright as day.
Leave your supper, and leave your sleep,
And come with your playfellows in the street.
Come with a whoop, come with a call,
Come with a good will or not at all.
Up the ladder and down the wall,
A halfpenny roll will serve us all.
You find milk and I'll find flour,
And we'll have a pudding in half an hour.

ℒULLABY

*H*ush, can you hear
in the thickening deep
the air in the trees
is falling asleep?

Hush, can you see
where the darkening skies
stretch over the sunset
and close heavy eyes?

Hush, can you hear
where the whispering corn
is settling down
and starting to yawn?

Hush, can you see
in the moon's silver beam
the light of the world
beginning to dream?

Hush, can you feel
the whole world give a sigh
and fall fast asleep
to your lullaby?

Barrie Wade

ROCK-A-BYE, BABY

Rock-a-bye, baby,
Thy cradle is green,
Father's a nobleman,
Mother's a queen.
And Betty's a lady
Who wears a gold ring,
And Johnny's a drummer,
And drums for the king.

The Sleeping Beauty

Adapted from Charles Perrault by Mary Finch

Once upon a time there was a king and queen who had a beautiful baby daughter. They asked all the fairies in the kingdom to her christening, hoping they would bring her special gifts. But there was one fairy they forgot to ask. She was very old and had not been seen in the kingdom for many years and they thought she was dead.

One by one, on the day of the christening, the fairies stepped forward to give the baby princess their gifts. The first gave her everlasting beauty, the second wished her a long and happy life, the third gave her wisdom, but just as the last fairy stepped forward with her magic wand there was a clap of thunder, a swirl of smoke and the very old fairy tottered into the hall.

"Why wasn't I invited to the christening?" she demanded. "I shall add my gift to the others, but you won't like it. When the princess is sixteen she will prick her finger on a spindle and fall down dead! Then you'll remember me!" And with that she vanished.

The poor king and queen were most upset, and the queen burst into tears, but at that moment the last fairy spoke.

"I can't undo the spell as my magic isn't strong enough, but I can change it. The princess will not die but she will fall asleep for a hundred years."

The king ordered all the spinning wheels and spindles in the kingdom to be thrown away, hoping to keep his daughter safe and the years passed. The princess grew up beautiful and happy and clever, but on her sixteenth birthday she wandered into a part of the palace she had never seen before, and into a little room where an old woman – who was the wicked fairy in disguise – was sitting spinning.

"What is that?" said the princess, who had, of course,

149

never seen a spinning wheel. "May I have a try?"

"Certainly," said the old woman, handing her the spindle, but the moment the princess touched it, she pricked her finger and fell down into a deep sleep. The fairy vanished, with a cackle of laughter.

The princess was carried into her bedroom and laid on her bed, and at that moment everyone in the palace fell asleep – the guards at the gate, the cooks in the kitchen and the king and queen on their thrones. Around the palace grew a thick prickly hedge and, as time went by, everyone in the surrounding countryside forgot that the palace was there.

Exactly one hundred years later a prince was riding through the country when he came to the thick hedge. Over the top of the hedge he could just see the turrets of a castle.

"What is that?" he asked his companions.

None of them knew, so the prince drew his sword and started to hack at the tangle of briars. As soon as his sword touched the hedge, it parted as if by magic and the prince was able to ride straight through it.

He soon came to the castle, where he found the guards asleep at the gate and everyone inside snoring where they sat. He wandered through the rooms, astonished, until he came to a bedroom.

There a princess lay asleep on her bed. He was so amazed by her beauty that he leant forward and kissed her, and at that moment she opened her eyes.

As she did so, everyone else started bustling around as if nothing had happened. The cooks stirred the soup, the dogs barked and the king and queen stretched on their thrones.

The princess smiled at the prince. "Thank you," she said. "You have saved me from a wicked spell. I have been asleep for a hundred years."

The prince married the princess and they lived happily together ever after, and to be on the safe side they didn't invite any fairies to the christenings of their babies.

THE SONG OF THE DAISY FAIRY

Come to me and play with me,
I'm the babies' flower;
Make a necklace gay with me,
Spend the whole long day with me,
Till the sunset hour.

I must say good-night, you know,
Till tomorrow's playtime;
Close my petals tight, you know,
Shut the red and white, you know,
Sleeping till the daytime.

Cicely Mary Barker

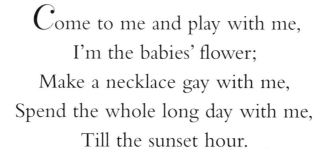

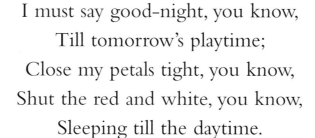

SLEEP, BABY, SLEEP

Sleep, baby, sleep.
Thy father guards the sheep;
Thy mother shakes the dreamland tree,
Down falls a little dream for thee;
Sleep, baby, sleep.
Sleep, baby, sleep.

Sleep, baby, sleep.
The large stars are the sheep;
The little stars are the lambs, I guess,
The gentle moon's the shepherdess;
Sleep, baby, sleep.
Sleep, baby, sleep.

Sleep, baby, sleep.
Thy father watches the sheep;
The wind is blowing fierce and wild.
It must not wake my little child;
Sleep, baby, sleep.
Sleep, baby, sleep.

BABY'S BOAT

Baby's boat's a silver moon
Sailing in the sky,
Sailing o'er a sea of sleep
While the stars float by.

Chorus
Sail, baby, sail
Out upon that sea;
Only don't forget to sail
Back again to me.

Baby's fishing for a dream,
Fishing far and near.
Her line a silver moonbeam is,
Her bait a silver star.

Chorus
Sail, baby, sail
Out upon that sea;
Only don't forget to sail
Back again to me.

Thomas Decker

VESPERS

Little boy kneels at the foot of the bed,
Droops on the little hands little gold head.
Hush! Hush! Whisper who dares!
Christopher Robin is saying his prayers.

God bless Mummy. I know that's right.
Wasn't it fun in the bath to-night?
The cold's so cold, and the hot's so hot.
Oh! God bless Daddy — I quite forgot.

If I open my fingers a little bit more,
I can see Nanny's dressing-gown on the door.
It's a beautiful blue, but it hasn't a hood.
Oh! God bless Nanny and make her good.

Mine has a hood, and I lie in bed,
And pull the hood right over my head,
And I shut my eyes, and I curl up small,
And nobody knows that I'm there at all.

Oh! Thank you, God, for a lovely day.
And what was the other I had to say?
I said "Bless Daddy", so what can it be?
Oh! Now I remember it. God bless Me.

Little boy kneels at the foot of the bed,
Droops on the little hands little gold head.
Hush! Hush! Whisper who dares!
Christopher Robin is saying his prayers

A. A. Milne

Baby Bunting

Bye, baby bunting,
Daddy's gone a-hunting,
Gone to get a rabbit skin
To wrap a baby bunting in.

LULLABY

It's my fat baby
I feel in my hood,
Oh, how heavy he is!
Ya ya! Ya ya!

When I turn my head
He smiles at me, my baby,
Hidden deep in my hood,
Oh, how heavy he is!
Ya ya! Ya ya!

How pretty he is when he smiles
With his two teeth, like a little walrus!
Oh, I'd rather my baby were heavy,
So long as my hood is full!

BEDTIME

Bedtime, bedtime,
Hot milk, honeyed-bread time,
Favourite book to read time,
Best rhymes to be said time,
Stairs quietly tread time,
Cosy bedspread time,
Cuddle with Ted time,
Eyes heavy as lead time,
Sleepy old head time.
Bedtime, bedtime.

John Kitching

THE
TALE OF
THE
FLOPSY
BUNNIES

BEATRIX POTTER

It is said that the effect of eating too much lettuce is "soporific".

I have never felt sleepy after eating lettuce; but then I am not a rabbit.

They certainly had a very soporific effect upon the Flopsy Bunnies!

When Benjamin Bunny grew up, he married his cousin Flopsy. They had a large family, and they were very improvident and cheerful.

I do not remember the separate names of their children; they were generally called the "Flopsy Bunnies".

As there was not always quite enough to eat,—Benjamin used to borrow cabbages from Flopsy's brother, Peter Rabbit, who kept a nursery garden.

Sometimes Peter Rabbit
had no cabbages to spare.

When this happened,
the Flopsy Bunnies
went across the field
to a rubbish heap, in
the ditch outside
Mr McGregor's garden.

Mr McGregor's rubbish
heap was a mixture.
There were jam pots
and paper bags, and
mountains of chopped
grass from the mowing
machine (which always
tasted oily), and some
rotten vegetable marrows
and an old boot or two.
One day—oh joy!—there
were a quantity of
overgrown lettuce,
which had "shot"
into flower.

The Flopsy Bunnies simply stuffed lettuce. By degrees, one after another, they were overcome with slumber, and lay down in the mown grass.

Benjamin was not so much overcome as his children. Before going to sleep he was sufficiently wide awake to put a paper bag over his head to keep off the flies.

The little Flopsy Bunnies slept delightfully in the warm sun. From the lawn beyond the garden came the distant clacketty sound of the mowing machine. The bluebottles buzzed about the wall and a little old mouse picked over the rubbish among the jam pots.

(I can tell you her name, she was called Thomasina Tittlemouse, a woodmouse with a long tail.)

She rustled across the paper bag and awakened Benjamin Bunny. The mouse apologized profusely, and said that she knew Peter Rabbit.

While she and Benjamin were talking, close under the wall, they heard a heavy tread above their heads; and suddenly Mr McGregor emptied out a sackful of lawn mowings right upon the top of the sleeping Flopsy Bunnies! Benjamin shrank down under his paper bag. The mouse hid in a jam pot.

The little rabbits smiled sweetly in their sleep under the shower of grass; they did not awake because the lettuce had been so soporific. They dreamt that their mother Flopsy was tucking them up in a hay bed.

Mr McGregor looked down after emptying his sack. He saw some funny little brown tips of ears sticking up through the lawn mowings. He stared at them for some time.

Presently a fly settled on one of them and it moved.

Mr McGregor climbed down on to the rubbish heap—

"One, two, three, four! five! six leetle rabbits!" said he as he dropped them into his sack. The Flopsy Bunnies dreamt that their mother was turning them over in bed. They stirred a little in their sleep, but still they did not wake up.

Mr McGregor tied up the sack and left it on the wall. He went to put away the mowing machine.

While he was gone,
Mrs Flopsy Bunny (who
remained at home) came
across the field.

She looked suspiciously
at the sack and wondered
where everybody was?

Then the mouse came
out of her jam pot, and
Benjamin took the paper
bag off his head, and they
told the doleful tale.

Benjamin and
Flopsy were in
despair, they
could not undo
the string.

But Mrs
Tittlemouse was
a resourceful
person. She
nibbled a hole
in the bottom
corner of
the sack.

The little rabbits were pulled out and pinched to wake them.

Their parents stuffed the empty sack with three rotten vegetable marrows, an old blacking-brush and two decayed turnips.

Then they all hid under a bush and watched for Mr McGregor.

Mr McGregor came back and picked up the sack, and carried it off.

He carried it hanging down, as if it were rather heavy.

The Flopsy Bunnies followed at a safe distance.

They watched him go into his house.

And then they crept up to the window to listen.

Mr McGregor threw down the sack on the stone floor in a way that would have been extremely painful to the Flopsy Bunnies, if they had happened to have been inside it.

They could hear him drag his chair on the flags, and chuckle—

"One, two, three, four, five, six leetle rabbits!" said Mr McGregor.

"Eh? What's that? What have they been spoiling now?" enquired Mrs McGregor.

"One, two, three, four, five, six leetle fat rabbits!" repeated Mr McGregor, counting on his fingers—"One, two, three—"

"Don't you be silly; what do you mean, you silly old man?"

"In the sack! one, two, three, four, five, six!" replied Mr McGregor.

(The youngest Flopsy Bunny got upon the window-sill.)

Mrs McGregor took hold of the sack and felt it. She said she could feel six, but they must be old rabbits, because they were so hard and all different shapes.

"Not fit to eat; but the skins will do fine to line my old cloak."

"Line your old cloak?" shouted Mr McGregor— "I shall sell them and buy myself baccy!"

"Rabbit tobacco! I shall skin them and cut off their heads."

Mrs McGregor untied the sack and put her hand inside.

When she felt the vegetables she became very very angry. She said that Mr McGregor had "done it a purpose."

And Mr McGregor was
very angry too. One of the
rotten marrows came flying
through the kitchen window,
and hit the youngest
Flopsy Bunny.

It was rather hurt.

Then Benjamin and Flopsy
thought that it was time to
go home.

So Mr McGregor
did not get his
tobacco, and Mrs
McGregor did not
get her rabbit skins.

But next Christmas Thomasina
Tittlemouse got a present of enough
rabbit-wool to make herself a cloak
and a hood, and a handsome muff
and a pair of warm mittens.

I Never See the Stars at Night

I never see the stars at night
waltzing round the Moon
without wondering why they dance
when no one plays a tune.

I hear no fiddles in the air
or high and heavenly band
but round about they dance, the stars
for ever hand in hand.

I think that wise ventriloquist
the Old Man in the moon
whistles so that only stars
can hear his magic tune.

George Barker

Sleep, Baby, Sleep

Sleep, baby, sleep!
Our cottage vale is deep;
The little lamb is on the green,
With woolly fleece so soft and clean.
Sleep, baby, sleep!

Sleep, baby, sleep!
Thy rest shall angels keep,
While on the grass the lamb shall feed,
And never suffer want or need.
Sleep, baby, sleep!

Sleep, baby, sleep!
Down where the woodbines creep;
Be always like the lamb so mild,
A kind, and sweet, and gentle child.
Sleep, baby, sleep!

SUMMER STARS

*B*end low again, night of summer stars.
So near, a long-arm man can pick off stars,
Pick off what he wants in the sky bowl,
So near, strumming, strumming,
So lazy and hum-strumming.

Carl Sandburg